SPORTS ALL-STARS

CRISTIANO RONALDO

Matt Doeden

Lerner Publications ◆ Minneapolis

Lerner Publications Company
A division of Lerner Publishing Group, Inc.
241 First Avenue North
Minneapolis, MN 55401 USA

For reading levels and more information, look up this title at www.lernerbooks.com.

Main body text set in Albany Std 15/22. Typeface provided by Agfa.

Library of Congress Cataloging-in-Publication Data

Names: Doeden, Matt, author.
Title: Cristiano Ronaldo / Matt Doeden.
Description: Minneapolis : Lerner Publications, [2016] | Series: Sports All-Stars | Includes bibliographical references and index. | Audience: Ages: 7–11. | Audience: Grades: 4 to 6.
Identifiers: LCCN 2016020550 (print) | LCCN 2016028606 (ebook) | ISBN 9781512425826 (lb : alk. paper) | ISBN 9781512431193 (pb : alk. paper) | ISBN 9781512428261 (eb pdf)
Subjects: LCSH: Ronaldo, Cristiano, 1985-–Juvenile literature. | Soccer players—Portugal—Biography—Juvenile literature.
Classification: LCC GV942.7.R626 D64 2016 (print) | LCC GV942.7.R626 (ebook) | DDC 796.334092 [B] —dc23

LC record available at https://lccn.loc.gov/2016020550

Manufactured in the United States of America
3-45376-23294-2/8/2018

CONTENTS

RECORD-BREAKER

Cristiano Ronaldo is one of the best scorers in soccer history.

In March 2015, Cristiano Ronaldo made soccer history. All eyes were on the Real Madrid **forward** as he and his teammates faced off with FC Schalke 04, a German team. The superstar had 74 career **Champions League** goals. That was just one shy of the all-time record.

No one doubted Ronaldo's talent. Many fans thought he was the greatest soccer player in the world. Some called him the best of all time. His quick feet and striking power made him a threat to score from anywhere on the **pitch**.

Ronaldo shouts after scoring a goal. His goal celebrations are a common sight at European soccer matches.

Yet the superstar wasn't popular with all soccer fans. Real Madrid followers loved him. Fans of other teams loved to boo him.

Real Madrid trailed in the 25th minute, 1–0. Ronaldo streaked toward the goal as the ball sailed through the air. He launched himself from the ground and knocked the ball into the net with his head. It was his 75th Champions League goal.

But he wasn't done yet. Real Madrid trailed, 2–1, just before halftime. Madrid's Fabio Coentrao passed the ball in front of the goal. Ronaldo was there again. He knocked in his second goal to tie the game.

FC Schalke 04 went on to win the game, 4–3. But Ronaldo had sealed his place in history. At just 30 years of age, he stood alone as the all-time leading scorer in Champions League play.

European soccer teams often have names that US fans may find unusual. FC Schalke 04's full team name is FC Gelsenkirchen–Schalke 04 e.V. Gelsenkirchen is the city in Germany where the team plays. The number 04 indicates that the team was founded in 1904.

OVERCOMING
THE ODDS

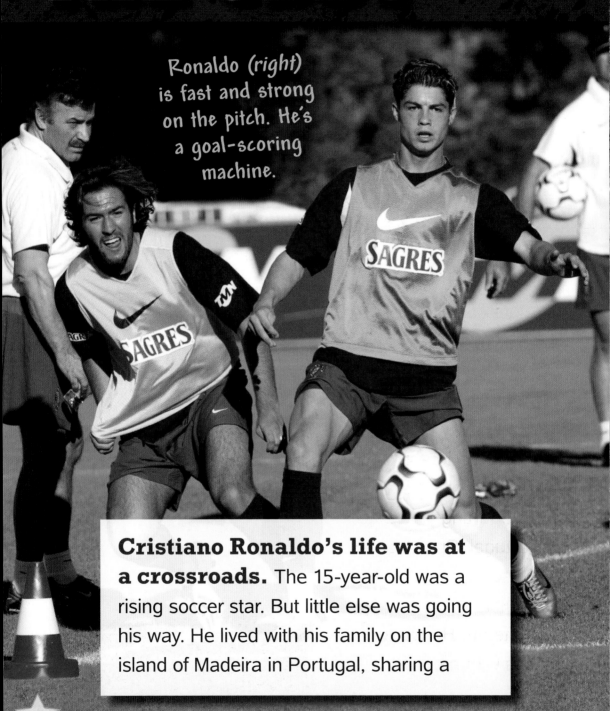

Ronaldo (right) is fast and strong on the pitch. He's a goal-scoring machine.

Cristiano Ronaldo's life was at a crossroads. The 15-year-old was a rising soccer star. But little else was going his way. He lived with his family on the island of Madeira in Portugal, sharing a room with his brother and two sisters. Just a year before, he'd been expelled from school.

Soccer was the highlight of Ronaldo's days. It had been his passion since childhood. His skills had already caught the attention of some of Europe's top soccer clubs. His track to the game's top ranks seemed clear. Then news came that threatened it all. Ronaldo had a heart problem. He needed surgery. His future of playing the game he loved was in doubt.

Ronaldo's surgery was a success. Within weeks, he was back on the pitch. A year later, in 2002, Ronaldo played for Sporting Clube de Portugal (Sporting CP). He scored two goals in his first game with the team. He wowed fans with his skills.

When he was a teenager, Ronaldo mostly played against older players.

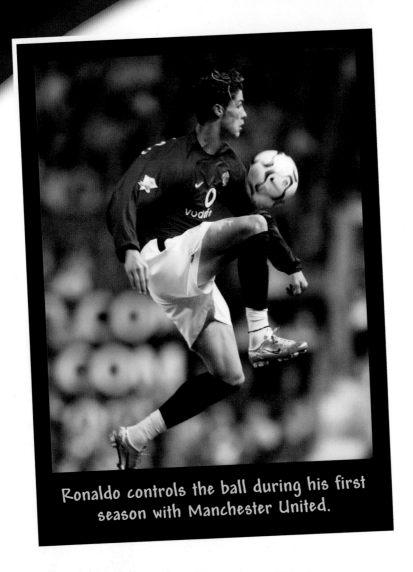

Ronaldo controls the ball during his first season with Manchester United.

Among the highlights for Sporting CP that season was a victory over the legendary Manchester United.

United manager Alex Ferguson took notice of Ronaldo. Before the 2003–2004 season, the young player signed a contract to play for United. It was worth about $17 million. The contract was the richest ever for a player so young. Ronaldo later called Ferguson "my father in sport, one of the most important factors and most influential in my career."

At first, Ronaldo struggled with his new team. Critics said he was trying too hard. They also thought he needed to pass the ball to his teammates more often. Yet his skills shined through. Ronaldo's biggest moment in his first season came in the biggest match of the year. United faced Millwall FC in the 2004 **FA Cup** final match. Ronaldo was dazzling. He scored the first goal of the game on a **header**. The play sparked United to a 3–0 win and the championship.

No one in soccer has faster feet than Ronaldo.

Ronaldo chats with Alex Ferguson during a
cold soccer practice.

Ferguson gushed about the 18-year-old star. "He's got a fantastic personality. He's got a great strength of mind. . . . I think those things will help him more than anything."

Ronaldo proved his manager right. By 2007–2008, many fans considered him the best player in the game. That season, he scored 42 goals in 49 matches, leading United to the Champions League title. He was awarded the Golden Shoe (or Golden Boot) as the top goal scorer in European soccer. Ronaldo was also a force in international play. He led Portugal to a fourth-place finish at the 2006 World Cup.

Yet all was not well. Fans questioned Ronaldo's commitment to Manchester. Rumors swirled that Ronaldo wanted to leave the team for new challenges and more money. In June 2009, it finally happened. Ronaldo transferred to Real Madrid of Spain and signed a huge new contract.

Ronaldo kept up his fierce scoring pace in La Liga, Spain's top league. He scored 100 goals in his first 92 games with Real Madrid. It was the fastest a player had reached 100 goals in La Liga history. In 2011–2012, he led his team to the league championship.

At the age of sixteen, Ronaldo still had a lot of growing to do.

Ronaldo is a fitness fanatic. When he started his pro soccer career, he was a skinny teenager. Since then, he has transformed his body, adding a lot of muscle. He credits his training, diet, and mental focus for his success.

Ronaldo trains three to four hours a day, five days a week. He starts with warmups to get loose, such as stretching and light running. From there, he moves to more intense **cardio** workouts and strength training. And of course, he does plenty of soccer drills. On his own, he works on his ball-control skills. He also practices with teammates to build teamwork.

Ronaldo adds variety to his training sessions. "Mix it up," he wrote in a list of training tips.

Ronaldo practices kicks during training. He works hard to make the most of his talent.

"I recommend a combination of cardio (running and rowing) and weight training to . . . increase both strength and stamina. [Mixing it up] also helps to keep it interesting."

Diet is another big part of Ronaldo's physical fitness. He tries to eat healthful foods and drink lots of water. His favorite foods include fish and steak. He avoids junk food. Ronaldo doesn't usually eat three big meals a day. Instead, he may eat six small meals. This keeps his body consistently fueled during the day.

Ronaldo drinks water throughout the day. He drinks even more during games.

Natural talent and physical fitness are only part of Ronaldo's success. "Mental strength is just as important as physical strength," he says. Ronaldo's focus is the key to his mental strength. He doesn't let himself stray from his routine. He starts with eight hours of sleep every night. Ronaldo doesn't stay up late partying. He keeps his mind sharp and focused by keeping it rested. He also avoids alcohol and drugs.

Goal setting is another way Ronaldo keeps on track. He challenges himself to meet personal fitness goals. His goals always give him something to work toward.

Stretching helps prevent injury.

Ronaldo is one of the world's most famous celebrities.

Ronaldo is an icon. He made his name on the soccer field. But he's also well known for his life off the field. His passion for fashion, his efforts for charity, and his high-profile love life have helped make him a household name.

Ronaldo has become almost as famous in the fashion world as he is in the soccer world. He has **endorsed** a wide range of clothing products. His good looks and athletic build make him a natural fit to model clothes. He even modeled underwear for clothing legend Armani.

In 2006, Ronaldo opened a clothing store called CR7. The store—named for Ronaldo's initials and jersey number—is on his home island of Madeira. Two years later, he opened another store in Lisbon, Portugal.

Fighting Back

Ronaldo is outspoken against the use of alcohol. His father died from liver damage that may have been caused by alcohol. In 2008, a newspaper falsely reported that Ronaldo had been drinking heavily. He sued the newspaper and won the lawsuit. But he didn't keep the money he'd won. He gave it all to charity.

Ronaldo stands in front of an advertisement for CR7.

In 2013, Ronaldo introduced his own clothing products. It started with CR7 Underwear. He helped to design the underwear and socks. A year later, Ronaldo expanded CR7 to include shirts and shoes. He vowed that his shoes would be made entirely in Portugal.

Ronaldo is involved with charities around the world. He remembers growing up with little money in Portugal, and he makes an effort to give back. In 2004, an earthquake and **tsunami** killed many people in nations along the Indian Ocean and Pacific Ocean. The tragedy hit home for Ronaldo. He was touched by the tale of a seven-year-old boy, Martunis, from Indonesia. The boy was stranded alone for three weeks. His mother and siblings had been killed. When rescuers found Martunis, he was wearing a Portugal soccer jersey.

Ronaldo donated money to help rebuild Martunis's home. He met with Martunis, and the two became friends. Eleven years later, Martunis signed with Sporting CP in Portugal. He joined the same team Ronaldo had once played for!

Ronaldo and Martunis posed for this photo in 2005.

Ronaldo has helped people in many other ways as well. In 2012, he paid for cancer treatments for a 10-month-old boy. And in 2013, he began working with Save the Children. His goal is to help end childhood hunger and promote healthful lifestyles.

Ronaldo's charity work makes headlines, but some European media spend even more time tracking his love life. His romantic relationships have included famous models Gemma Atkinson, Alice Goodwin,

Save the Children works to improve the health of kids around the world. Ronaldo joined the group in 2013.

Ronaldo poses with his son on the red carpet.

and Irina Shayk. In 2010, Ronaldo became a father. His son, nicknamed Cristianinho (little Cristiano), was born in June. Ronaldo never released the name of the boy's mother.

Ronaldo is a single dad to Cristianinho. The soccer superstar said that his son wants to follow in his dad's footsteps but with one difference. Cristianinho doesn't want to be a forward like his dad. He wants to be a goalkeeper.

This wax statue of Ronaldo stands at the CR7 Museum.

Ronaldo's status as a pop culture icon continues to grow. His popularity is unmatched on his home island of Madeira. In 2013, he opened CR7 Museum there. The museum houses Ronaldo's trophies, jerseys, and more. He has also been the subject of several films. Among them was the 2014 **documentary** *Cristiano Ronaldo: World at His Feet*. The film tells the superstar's life story. And in 2015, he set a record as the most liked person on Facebook!

In 2014, Ronaldo kissed the Golden Shoe, one of his many trophies.

Ronaldo also continues to expand his business. In 2015, he announced his own men's **fragrances**, called Legacy. The star says he helped select and shape each fragrance himself.

Ronaldo enjoys the spotlight off the field. But his focus remains on soccer. He has helped Real Madrid remain one of the top soccer clubs in Europe. The 2014–2015 season was one of his finest. Ronaldo scored a career-high 61 goals.

In 2015, Ronaldo became the leading scorer in Champions League history. He also became Real Madrid's all-time leading goal scorer. A year later, he booted in the winning goal to give Real Madrid the Champions League title. With every goal he scores,

In 2016, Forbes magazine said Ronaldo was the highest-paid athlete in the world. The magazine predicted he would earn about $88 million that year.

Ronaldo's case as the best player of his generation grows. And many fans believe that by the time he hangs up his shoes, he'll be remembered as the greatest soccer player of all time.

Ronaldo (right), despite his fame and fortune, has not lost sight of his main goal: winning soccer matches.

- 2 Eusébio
- 2 Gerd Müller
- 2 Dudu Georgescu
- 2 Fernando Gomes
- 2 Ally McCoist
- 2 Mário Jardel
- 2 Thierry Henry
- 2 Diego Forlán
- 2 Luis Suárez

Most Goals in La Liga History (through May 14, 2016)

- 312 Lionel Messi
- 260 Cristiano Ronaldo
- 251 Telmo Zarra
- 234 Hugo Sánchez
- 228 Raúl

Source Notes

10 "Ronaldo Vows to Justify Price Tag," *BBC*, last modified July 4, 2009, http://news.bbc.co.uk/sport2 /hi/football/teams/m/man_utd/8134301.stm.

12 "Manchester United Win FA Cup Final," *CNN*, May 22, 2004, http://edition.cnn.com/2004/SPORT /football/05/22/england.cup.

16 Jack Briden, "Cristiano Ronaldo Reveals 'Top 15 Fitness Tips' to Get a Body Like His . . . but Alcohol Is Forbidden and You'll Need an Early Night!," *Daily Mail* (UK), February 6, 2015, http://www.dailymail .co.uk/sport/football/article-2942526/Cristiano -Ronaldo-reveals-15-health-fitness-tips-body-like -alcohol-forbidden-ll-need-early-night.html.

17 Ibid.

Glossary

cardio: a type of workout designed to get the heart pumping and improve blood flow

Champions League: a yearly competition between Europe's top soccer teams

documentary: a film that presents factual information, rather than a scripted plot

endorsed: supported and appeared in advertisements for a company or product

FA Cup: a yearly competition between the top soccer teams in England

forward: a position in soccer. Forwards are usually responsible for attacking the other team's goal.

fragrances: perfumes or aftershaves

header: a shot or pass made by hitting the ball with the head

pitch: a soccer field

tsunami: a large, powerful wave, usually caused by an earthquake

Further Information

CR7—Official Website of Cristiano Ronaldo
http://www.cristianoronaldo.com

Fishman, Jon M. *Alex Morgan*. Minneapolis: Lerner Publications, 2016.

Jökulsson, Illugi. *Cristiano Ronaldo*. New York: Abbeville Kids, 2015.

SI Kids—Soccer
http://www.sikids.com/soccer

Torres, John Albert. *Soccer Star Cristiano Ronaldo*. Berkeley Heights, NJ: Speeding Star, 2014.

Index

Photo Acknowledgments

The images in this book are used with the permission of: © iStockphoto.com/iconeer (gold stars); © Manuel Queimadelos Alonso/Getty Images, p. 1; © Alex Grimm/Bongarts/Getty Images, p. 6; © ANTONIO COTRIM/AFP/Getty Images, p. 8; © VI Images/Getty Images, pp. 9, 14; © Laurence Griffiths/Getty Images, p. 10; © ADRIAN DENNIS/AFP/Getty Images, p. 11; © Matthew Peters/Manchester United/Getty Images, p. 12; © ALEXANDER NEMENOV/AFP/Getty Images, p. 15; © Jasper Juinen/Getty Images, p. 16; © GENT SHKULLAKU/AFP/Getty Images, p. 17; © Jack Taylor/AFP/Getty Images, p. 18; © David Ramos for CR7/Getty Images, p. 20; © FRANCISCO PARAISO/AFP/Getty Images, p. 21; ZCVA WENN Photos/Newscom, p. 22; © Karwai Tang/WireImage/Getty Images, p. 23; © GREGORIO CUNHA/AFP/Getty Images, p. 24; PABLOGARCIA/MARCA/SIPA/Newscom, p. 25; © Catherine Ivill/AMA/Getty Images, p. 27.

Front cover: © Manuel Queimadelos Alonso/Getty Images; © iStockphoto.com/neyro2008 (motion lines); © iStockphoto.com/ulimi (black and white stars).